a stuck truck

a sleeping fireman

FIRE HOUSE

RITZ APARTMENTS

HARDWARE

window washer

BARBER SHOP

laundress

delivery boy

AUTOMOBILES

Some workers always do their
work at the same place.

automobile salesman

TELEPHONE
BOOTH

Others travel from place
to place to do their jobs.
What does your Daddy do?
What does your Mommy do?

jack
hammer

TAXI

And what do YOU do?
Are you a good helper?

ditch digger

5

# Everyone is a worker

Farmer Alfalfa

Blacksmith Fox

Stitches the tailor

Grocer Cat    Mommy    Huckle

How many workers are there here?
One, two, three, four, five, six.
What do these workers do?

Hi Daddy!

Farmer Alfalfa grows all kinds of food.
He keeps some of it for his family.

He sells the rest to Grocer Cat
in exchange for money.
Grocer Cat will sell the food
to other people in Busytown.

GROCERIES

Potatoes

Today Alfalfa bought a new suit
with some of the money he got
from Grocer Cat.
Stitches, the tailor, makes clothes.
Alfalfa bought his new suit from Stitches.

Then Alfalfa went to Blacksmith Fox's
shop. He had saved enough money
to buy a new tractor. The new tractor
will make his farm work easier.
With it he will be able to grow
more food than he could grow before.
He also bought some presents for
Mommy and his son, Alfred.

Alfalfa put the rest of the money
in the bank for safekeeping.
Then he drove home to his family.

Mommy loved her new earrings.
Alfred loved his present, too.

What did the other workers do with the money they earned?
First they bought food to eat
and clothes to wear.
Then, they put some of the money
in the bank. Later they will use
the money in the bank
to buy other things.

What else did they buy?
Stitches bought an egg beater
so that his family could make fudge.
Try not to get any on your new clothes!

How do I look?

iron

sand bag

bellows

forge

Blacksmith Fox bought more iron
for his shop.
He will heat and bend the metal
to make more tractors and tools.

Grocer Cat bought a new dress for Mommy.
She earned it by taking such good care
of the house.
He also bought a present for his son, Huckle.
Huckle was a very good helper today.

# Building a new house

Huckle lived with his Mommy and Daddy in a part of Busytown where there were no other houses nearby. There were no other children to play with.
Huckle was very lonely.

Then one day a man came and dug a hole in the empty lot next door. Someone was going to build a new house. Huckle wondered if there would be any children in the new family.

Jason, the mason, made a foundation
in the hole for the house to be built on.
His helper mixed cement
to hold the bricks together.

Sawdust, the carpenter, and his helpers
started to build the frame of the house.
Jason started to build a chimney.

I wonder if any children
will live there?

Jake, the plumber, attached the water
and sewer pipes to the main pipes
under the street.

10

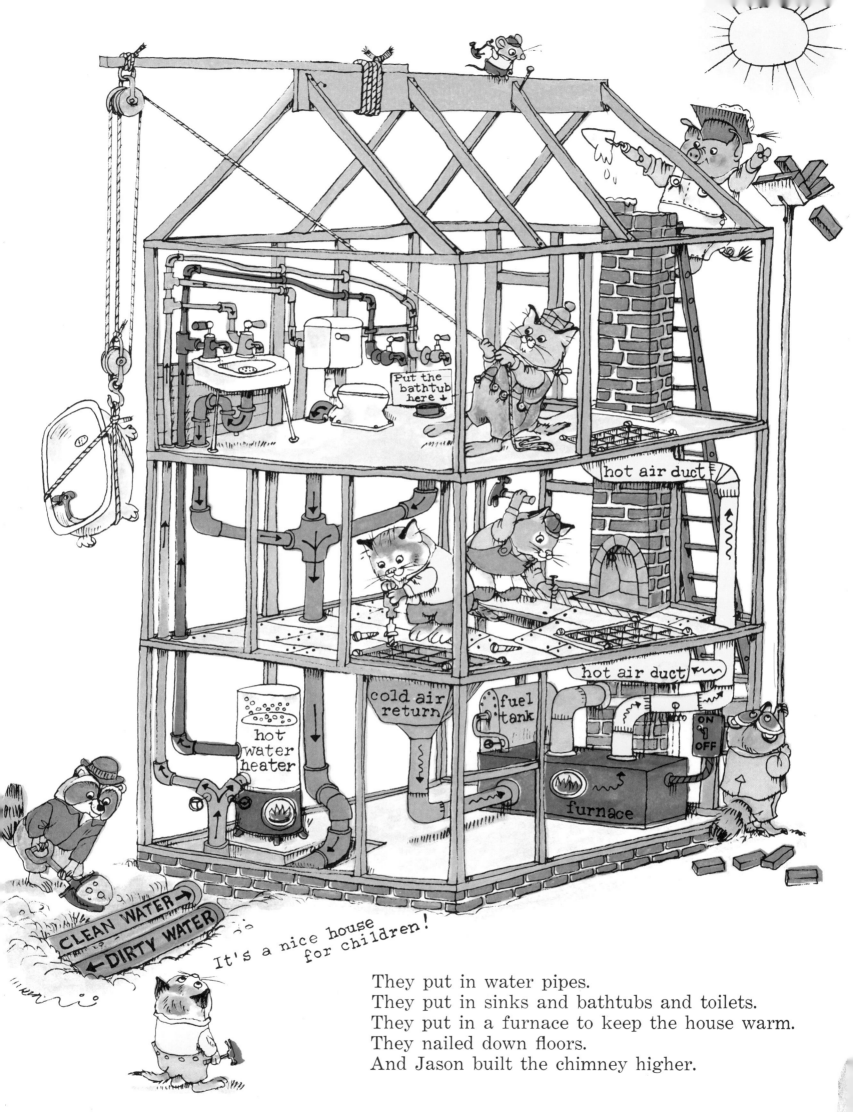

Put the bathtub here ↓

hot air duct

hot air duct

cold air return

fuel tank

hot water heater

furnace

ON OFF

CLEAN WATER →
← DIRTY WATER

It's a nice house for children!

They put in water pipes.
They put in sinks and bathtubs and toilets.
They put in a furnace to keep the house warm.
They nailed down floors.
And Jason built the chimney higher.

11

Jason finished making the chimney.
Be careful you don't fall, Jason!

electricity and telephone utility pole

fuse box

NEVER, NEVER
TOUCH!

They put a roof and sides on the house.
The electrician put in electric wires.
All kinds of telephones were put in.

12

The electrician attached electric
switches and outlets to the wires.

Sawdust nailed up the inside walls.
The walls covered up all the pipes and wires.

He put windows
where they belonged—and doors, too.

The house was painted
inside and outside.

stove

sink

refrigerator

clothes washer

A truck brought furniture, a television set,
a radio, rugs, pictures, a stove and lots of other
things. The house was ready for the new family.

At last the new family has arrived!
Look! It is Stitches, the tailor!
Stitches paid the workmen for
building the house.

bag of money

13

And here is Stitches' family.
"Look, children," said Mother Stitches.
"We have found a new playmate for you."
And Huckle was never lonesome after that.

14

# Mailing a letter

Betsy Bear wrote a letter to Grandma to wish her a Happy Birthday.

She went to the post office to mail it.

She bought an airmail stamp and stuck it on the envelope.

She put the letter in the letter slot.

The postmen stamp all the letters with an inked postmark stamp.

The ink postmark tells you the name of the town that the letter was mailed from. The address shows where the letter is to go.

127,963
127,964

Uncle Benny, the postmaster, read the address on each letter. All the neighboring towns have cubbyholes in Busytown Post Office. Uncle Benny put all the letters that were going to Grandma's town in one cubbyhole. He put the letters going to other towns in different cubbyholes.

Then he put all the letters that were going to Grandma's town in a mailbag.

He took it to Busytown Airport and put it on an airplane.

Off to Grandma's town the airplane flew.
A postman was waiting at the airport.
He took the mailbag to Grandma's
Post Office.

He read the address on each letter
to see to what part of town it was
to be sent. Each letter carrier
delivers letters to a different
part of town.

Soon the bag of Zip, the letter carrier,
was stuffed full. There was no more room
for the last letter, so he put it in his hat.

17

STOP! STOP!
Where is my birthday letter?

Sorry, Grandma

Grandma was waiting for a birthday
letter from Betsy.

But Zip walked right past
her house! He said he didn't
have a letter for Grandma in his bag.

She asked him to
please look again.
So he did.

No! Sorry! No letter for Grandma.
He tipped his hat "Good-bye"
—and a letter fell out!
It was Betsy's letter to Grandma!

"Why Zip! You dear postman!" she said.
"You DID bring me a letter from my
granddaughter after all!"

She was so happy that she gave Zip a big kiss.
Grandmothers just LOVE to get letters
from their grandchildren!

Happy Birthday
Grandma
Love and
Kisses xxx
Betsy

18

# Firemen to the rescue

FIRE!
Mother Cat was ironing
one of Daddy's shirts.
The iron was too hot.
The shirt began to burn.
"FIRE!" she shouted.

Davy Dog went to the
fire-alarm box. He pulled
the knob that sounded
the alarm at the fire house.

Firemen are at the fire house
at all times. They have to be
ready to put fires out quickly.

As soon as the alarm rang,
they ran to their fire engines.
HURRY!

LOCATION OF
ALARM BOXES

Hurry!

19

*Clang! Clang! Clang!*
The firemen rushed to the fire.
They raised the ladder on the ladder truck.
A fireman ran up the ladder to rescue Mommy.
"SAVE MY HUCKLE!" she screamed.

water hydrant

Save Huckle too!

Water is used to put fires out.
The water runs through pipes under the street.
The firemen attached a hose between the
water hydrant and the pumper engine.
The pumper engine got water from the hydrant
and squirted it out through the hose nozzle.

But the ladder wasn't
long enough to reach Huckle
up in the playroom!
How will they ever save him?

"SAVE MY HUCKLE!" screamed Mommy Cat as the firemen carried her down.

Smokey came running to the house.
He had a smoke mask so that
he would be able to breathe
in the smoke-filled house.
He also had a special ladder.

He climbed up the
fire-truck ladder
as far as he could.
He reached up with
his special ladder
and hooked it over
the window sill. Then he
climbed up.
He just had to
rescue Huckle!

The playroom door was closed.
Smokey chopped it down with his ax.

He picked up Huckle—
and he jumped out the window!

PLOPP!
Sparky and Snozzle were ready
just in time to catch them
in the life net.
Daddy arrived just in time
to see Smokey save Huckle.

At last the fire was out.
Look at poor Daddy's shirt!
But that doesn't matter.
The firemen have saved
his family and his house.
That is much more important!

The firemen went back to the fire house.
They hung the wet hose up to dry.
They put a fresh, dry hose on the trucks.
They have to be ready to fight fires
ALL OF THE TIME!
Brave firemen are always ready
to protect us and our homes from fire.

Hey!
Smokey!
Why didn't you
just OPEN the
playroom door?

# A visit to the hospital

Mommy took Abby to visit Doctor Lion.
He looked at her tonsils.
"Hmmmm. Very bad tonsils," he said.
"I shall have to take them out.
Meet me at the hospital tomorrow."

On the next day, Daddy drove them to the hospital.
Abby waved to the ambulance driver.
Ambulances bring people to hospitals
if they have to get there in a hurry.

Nurse Nelly was waiting for Abby.
Mommy had to go home, but she
promised to bring Abby a present
after the doctor had taken her
tonsils out.

25

Nurse Nelly took Abby up to the children's room.

Roger Dog was in the bed next to hers.
His tonsils were already out.
He was eating a big dish of ice cream.

Nurse Nelly put Abby on the bed.
She pulled a curtain around them.
No one could see what was going on.

Why, she was helping Abby
put on a nightgown!

Doctor Lion peeked into the room.
He told Nurse Nelly he was going
to put on his operating clothes.
He told Nurse Nelly to bring
Abby to the operating room.

Off to the operating room they went.
Doctor Lion was waiting there.
Everyone but the patient wears
a face mask in the operating room
so that germs won't spread.

Doctor Lion told Abby that she
was going to go to sleep.
He said she would stay asleep
until her tonsils were out.

Doctor Dog put a mask
over her nose and mouth.
She breathed in and out.
In an instant she was asleep.

When she woke up she found
herself back in the bed next
to Roger's. Her tonsils were all gone!
Her throat was sore, but it felt better
after she had some ice cream.

*Whooooeeee!*
Abby saw her Mommy arriving
in the ambulance.
Abby thought her mother must be
in a hurry to see her.

*Hurry!*

27

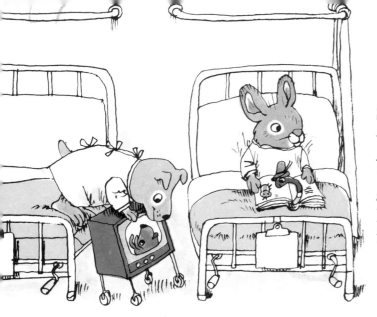

She waited and waited
—but Mommy didn't come.
At last Doctor Lion came.
"Your Mother has brought you
a present," he said.
He took Abby for a ride
in a wheelchair.

"There is your present," he said.
"It is your new baby brother!
Your mother just gave birth to
him here in the hospital."
Then they all went to Mommy's
room in the hospital.
Daddy was there, too.

What a lucky girl she was!
She left her tonsils
at the hospital,
but she brought home
a cute baby brother.

He looks like me, don't you think?

But remember! Very few children receive such
a nice present when they have their tonsils out!

# The train trip

The Pig family is going on a train
to visit their cousins in a town far away.
They will travel all day and all night to get there.

Daddy buys train tickets
at the railroad station.

Mommy buys books
and magazines to read.

A porter takes their bags
to the train.

This old train has a steam locomotive.
It is only going to make
a short trip to the next town.
The Pig family will ride
overnight on another train.

Wait! HALT!

Their train has a sleeping car
with separate rooms for each family.
These rooms are called compartments.
At night, the seats will be made into beds.
Look! There is Huckle's family.

Food and water is brought to
the kitchen in the dining car.
The cook will cook their meals.
The waiter will serve them.

ALL ABOOOOOARD!
It is time to leave.
The train rolls out of the station.
The signal light tells the engineer
that there is a clear track ahead.
He doesn't want to bump into another train.

signal tower

Mailbags and heavy baggage
are put on the train.
Some of it will be delivered
to stations along the way.

The locomotive needs fuel oil
to make its motors go.
The motors turn the wheels so that
the train can roll along the railroad track.

The switchman can
switch the train
from one track to another.
If he makes a mistake
the train won't go
to the right place.

The conductor collects the tickets. The tickets show that Daddy has paid for the trip.

In Huckle's compartment, the porter is getting the pillows and blankets ready for bedtime.

It is time to eat dinner.
Cookie has already made the soup.
He is trying to flip the pancakes
from the side that is cooked
to the side that is not cooked.
You are not doing very well, Cookie!

The mailman delivers a bag of mail to the railroad station of a town they are passing through.

The watchman lowers the crossing
gates before a train crosses a road.
He doesn't want any cars to
bump into the train.
But Wild Bill Hiccup
just HAS to bump into something!

Oh dear!
The train has swerved and the
waiter has spilled the soup!

While they are eating,
the porter changes
their seats into beds.

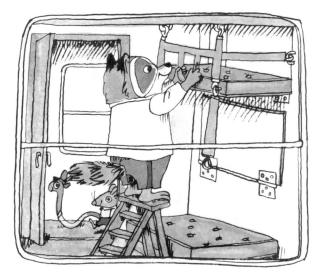

NICHT STÖREN
NE PAS
DÉRANGER
NON DISTURBARE
DON'T DISTURB

After dinner, everyone gets ready for bed.

*Clickety clack, clickety clack.*
The train speeds on through the night.
The train crew won't go to sleep
until the trip is over.
Cookie is still trying to learn how to
flip pancakes. Keep trying, Cookie.

WIENER
SCHNITZEL

ICE CREAM CAR

It is morning when they
arrive at their cousin's town.
Their cousins are at the
railroad station to greet them.
I think they will have fun
on their visit. Don't you?

# The story of seeds
## and how they grow

Farmer Alfalfa grows all kinds of vegetables on his farm.

Best of all, he likes to grow sweet, sweet corn.

Last summer when it was time to plant corn, Alfalfa poured the bag of corn seeds into the corn planter. Don't spill!

He planted the seeds in straight rows in his cornfield.

The hot sun shone down and after a while, tiny green plants popped up.
The corn was starting to grow.

Rain fell on the plants. Soon ears of corn grew on the cornstalks.

Then—after many days of sun and rain—
Alfalfa opened an ear of corn.
He wanted to see if his field of corn
was ready to be picked.
It was! The corn was ripe and ready for eating.

Alfalfa drove his corn picker
back and forth across his cornfield.
The ears of corn were picked from
the stalks and dumped into a wagon.

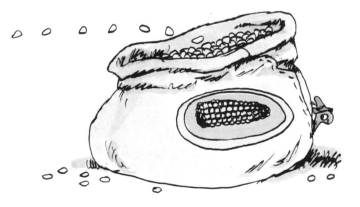

Each ear of corn has many seed kernels.
Alfalfa knew that he would need seeds to plant
at the next corn-planting time.
So he put some corn kernels in a bag
to save for planting.
He kept some ears to eat himself.

He put the rest in his
little old truck to sell to Grocer Cat.
My! His truck is falling apart!

Well, that's the end of THAT truck!
Grocer Cat gave money to Alfalfa for the corn.

With the money he earned growing corn,
Alfalfa bought a shiny new truck.
The Pig family went to Grocer Cat's store.
Pigs just love corn!

They bought lots of corn and took it home for supper.

They ate and ate and ate
until there was no more left
—except one tiny little seed corn!
Mommy Pig said to Harry,
"FINISH YOUR SUPPER!"

Harry asked if he could plant
the last tiny seed instead of
eating it. Mommy agreed.
He planted the seed in the earth.
The sun shone hot and the rain fell cool.
After a while, a tiny green plant popped up.
The plant grew and grew and grew.

One day Alfalfa came to visit.
"My goodness," he said.
"Harry has grown the best
corn I have ever seen.
I am sure he will grow up
to be a very good farmer!"
Harry was very pleased.

# Wood
## and how we use it

We couldn't live without trees.
We get wood from trees.
We use wood in many ways.
Let's see how we get our wood.

TIMBER!

The lumberjack cuts down the tree.

The branches are cut
off the tree trunk.

The tree trunk is sawed into logs.

tree
trunk

a seed

a one year old tree

log

This tree is almost 100 years old
and is ready to be cut down

The logs are put
in a river to
float downstream.

40

The forest ranger watches out
for fires. A forest fire
could burn down a whole forest.

Some trees are left standing.
Seeds from these trees
will fall to the ground.
New trees will grow in place of
the old ones that have been cut down.

The foresters also
scatter seeds from helicopters.

stump

Loggers ride the logs down the river.
They try to keep the logs from getting jammed.
Oh dear! The logs are jammed!
Unscramble that log jam, loggers!

Good work, loggers!
You broke up the log jam.
Now the logs can float to
the sawmill and be sawed into boards.

TOM SAWYER'S SAWMILL

Water falling over
a water wheel makes
all the machinery work.

lumber

lumberyard

SAWDUST THE CARPENTER

BOAT BUILDER

FURNITURE

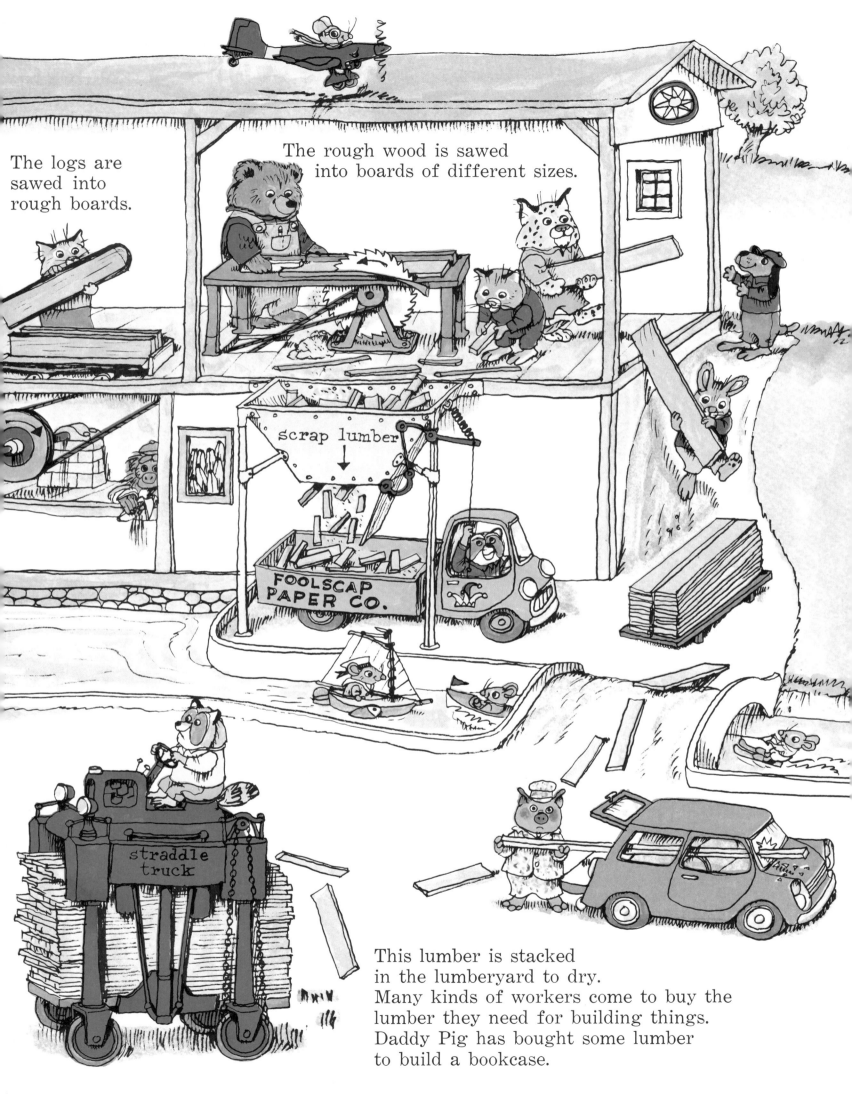

The logs are sawed into rough boards.

The rough wood is sawed into boards of different sizes.

scrap lumber

FOOLSCAP PAPER CO.

straddle truck

This lumber is stacked in the lumberyard to dry.
Many kinds of workers come to buy the lumber they need for building things.
Daddy Pig has bought some lumber to build a bookcase.

43

The paper makers use scraps
of wood to make paper.

FOOLSCAP
PAPER
COMPANY

chipper

blower

digester

chemicals

beater

mixer

Wet wood pulp moves onto a wire screen belt.
Water is removed by rollers and dryers.

dry end | drying | paper making machine | wire screen | wet end | wet wood pulp

a finished
roll of paper

ABC
PRINTERS

Some paper is used to make bags and boxes.
Some is for making books.
The paper used in this book was taken
to the printing shop where books are made.
The printer put the words
and pictures on the pages.

The boat builder uses curved
pieces of wood to make boats.

BOAT BUILDER

44

FURNITURE MAKER

lathe

jig saw

SAWDUST THE CARPENTER

The furniture maker makes beds and chests and chairs.

FURNITURE

Carpenters have a custom of nailing a tree branch to the roof of a new house.

Some trees give us fruit.

POLLY  JAN

MA  PA

D.J.  D.C.

NEWS
GREAT Plumbing and Heating Problems at the Rectory house. More later.

ICE CREAM

Trees shade us from the hot sun.

Harry is planting an apple seed.
An apple tree will grow from the seed.
It will take a long time.
Someday YOU might like to plant a tree.

# Building a new road

Good roads are very important to all of us.
Doctors need them to visit patients.
Firemen need them to go to fires.
We all need them to visit one another.
The road between Busytown and Workville
was bumpy and crooked and very dusty—

—except when it rained!
Then the dirt turned to mud and everyone got stuck.

The mayors of the two towns went to the road engineer
and told him that they wanted to have a new road.
The townspeople had agreed to pay the road engineer
and his workers to build the new road.

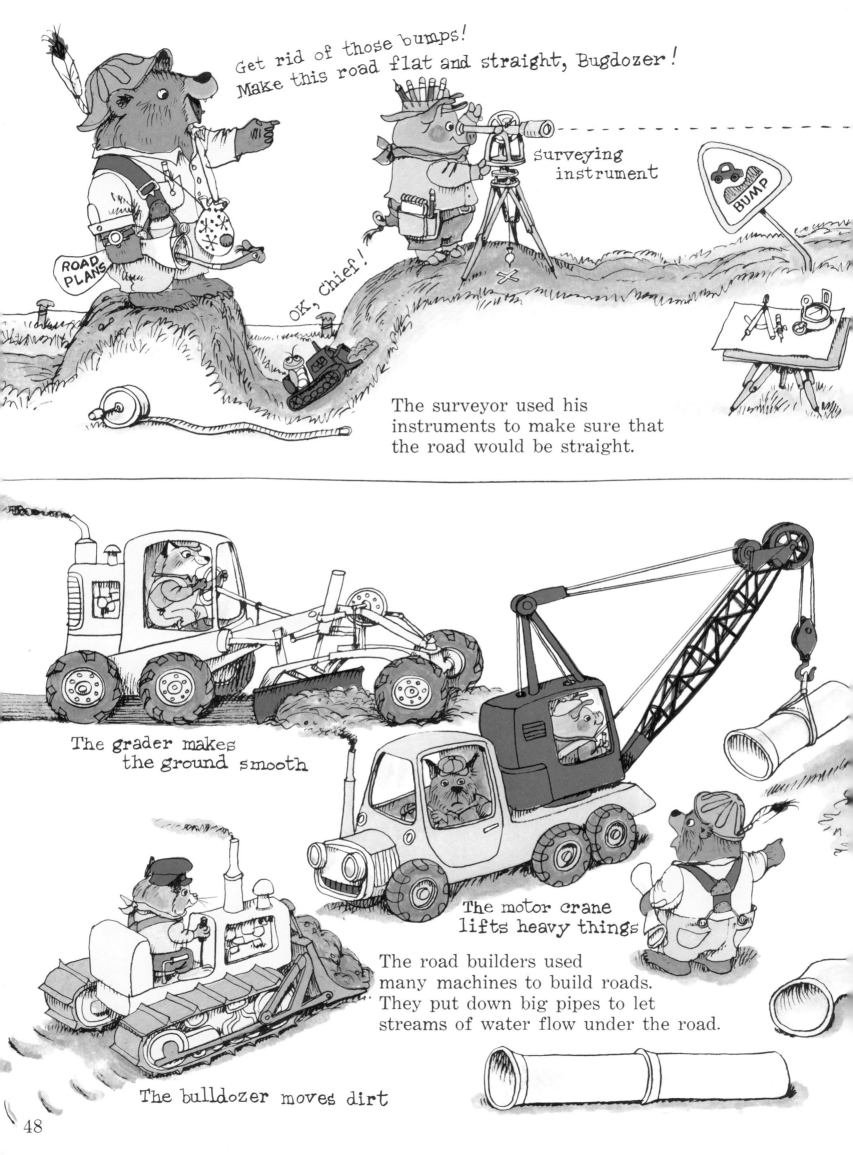

Get rid of those bumps!
Make this road flat and straight, Bugdozer!

OK, Chief!

surveying instrument

ROAD PLANS

BUMP

The surveyor used his instruments to make sure that the road would be straight.

The grader makes the ground smooth

The motor crane lifts heavy things

The bulldozer moves dirt

The road builders used many machines to build roads. They put down big pipes to let streams of water flow under the road.

The surveyor's helpers used stakes and string to show where the road was to go.

water drainage ditch

tractor shovel

ditch digger

dump truck

At last the roadbed was
straight and smooth.
But it needed a hard top
so that there would be no dust or mud.

power
shovel

rock crusher

Big rocks were put into the rock crusher
to be crushed into smaller stones.

A stone spreader spread the stones
evenly over the roadbed.

ASPHALT
OIL
SPREADER

dump
truck

stone spreader

A truck squirted sticky asphalt oil
on the stones to make them stick together.

keystone

The stone cutter shapes
the stones so that they
will fit next to each other

The asphalt mixer made hot, sticky asphalt.

The asphalt was poured into
the level finisher, which
spread it out flat on the road.

A heavy roller
pressed down the asphalt
to make it smooth and hard.

The road was built high in the middle
so that rain water would roll off
into ditches at the sides.

How am I doing,
Chief?

Street lights were put up so that drivers could see the road clearly at night.

FIREFLY LIGHTING COMPANY

electric cable

SNACK BAR

EAT

GASOLINE

gas pump

GAS AND OIL

OIL OIL OIL
OIL OIL OIL

gasoline storage tank

DIVIDING LINE PAINTER

GARDENER

All right, you two fellows! Stop talking and finish covering up that underground gasoline storage tank!

The workers put up guard rails
to keep cars from going off the road.

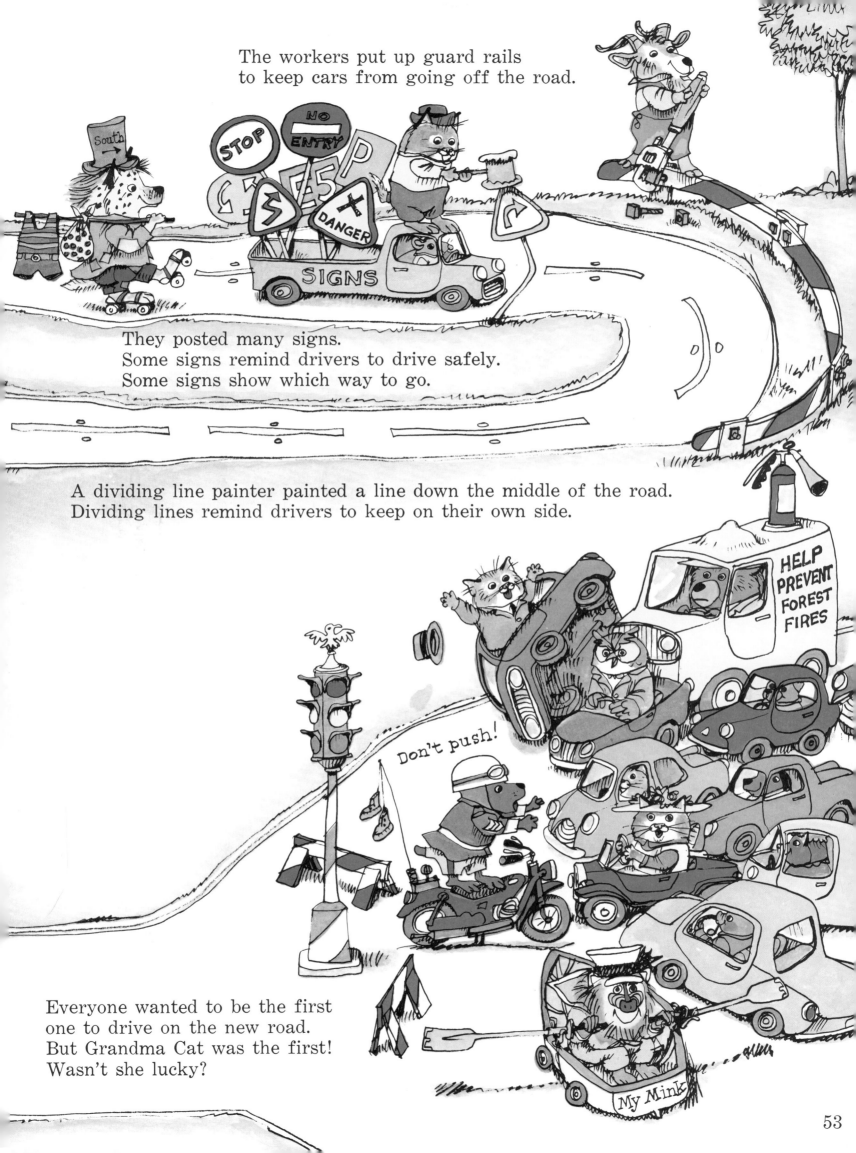

They posted many signs.
Some signs remind drivers to drive safely.
Some signs show which way to go.

A dividing line painter painted a line down the middle of the road.
Dividing lines remind drivers to keep on their own side.

Don't push!

Everyone wanted to be the first
one to drive on the new road.
But Grandma Cat was the first!
Wasn't she lucky?

# A voyage on a ship

the ship's painter

IRISH PENNANT

cargo boom

cargo winch

dock

KEEP OFF

NUTS

FUEL OIL

WATER

APPLES

EGGS
FRESH DAILY

BREAD

CHEESE

MAIL

MAIL

Captain Salty and his crew are getting
their ship ready for a voyage.
The ship will carry passengers to visit
their friends in a faraway land
across the ocean.

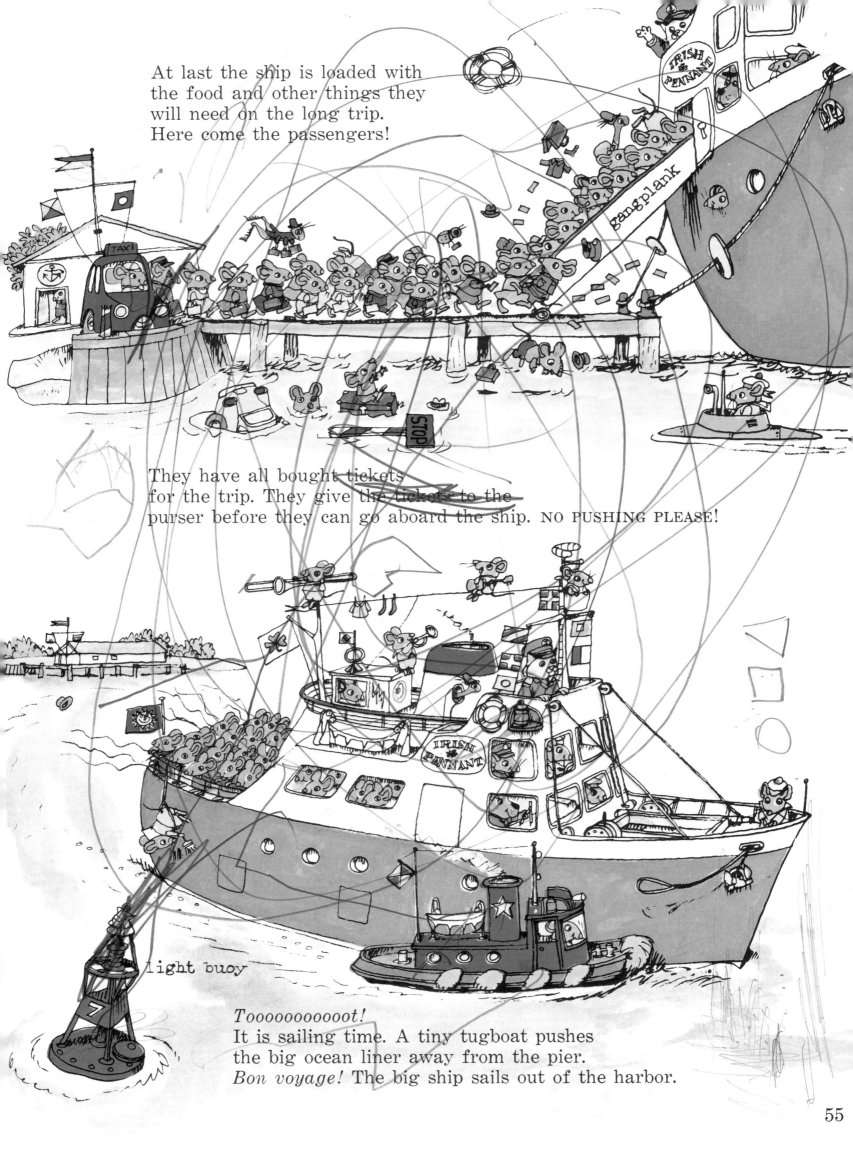

At last the ship is loaded with
the food and other things they
will need on the long trip.
Here come the passengers!

They have all bought tickets
for the trip. They give the tickets to the
purser before they can go aboard the ship. NO PUSHING PLEASE!

gangplank

STOP

light buoy

7

*Tooooooooooot!*
It is sailing time. A tiny tugboat pushes
the big ocean liner away from the pier.
*Bon voyage!* The big ship sails out of the harbor.

IRISH PENNANT

55

Soon it is crossing the wide ocean.
There is no land in sight.
Just look at all the things that
happen on an ocean-going ship!

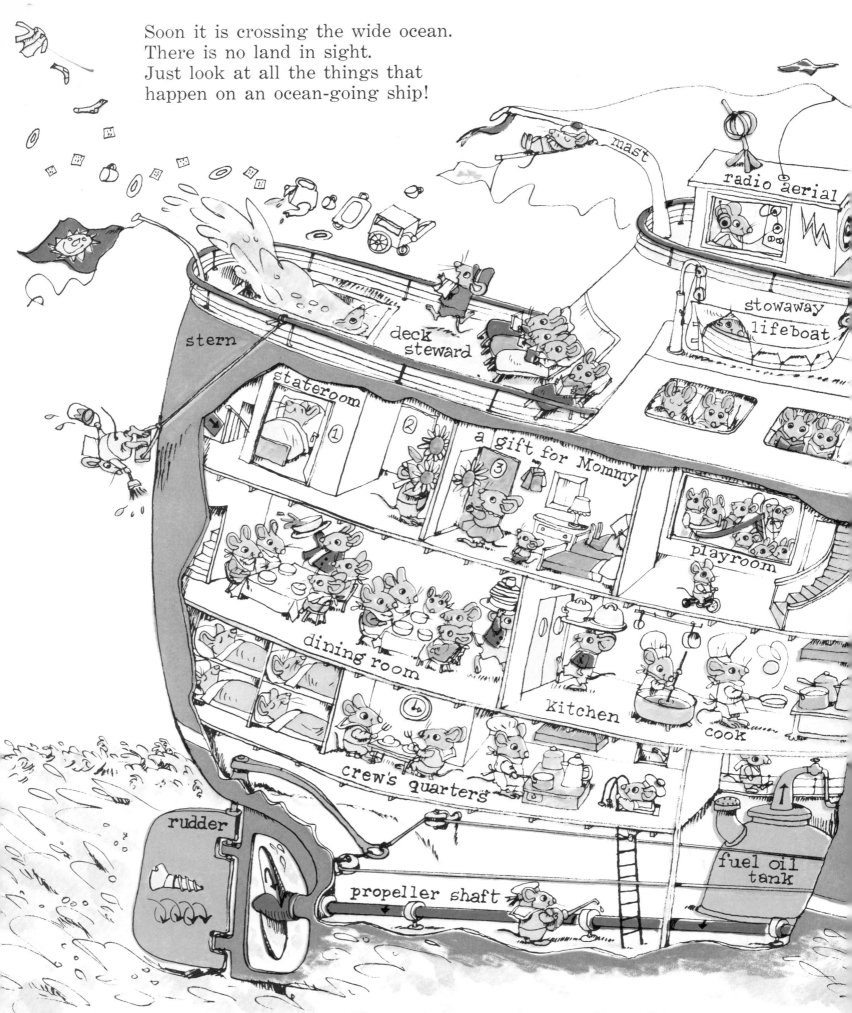

mast

radio aerial

stowaway
lifeboat

stern

deck
steward

stateroom

① ②

③

a gift for Mommy

playroom

dining room

kitchen

cook

crew's quarters

rudder

propeller shaft

fuel oil
tank

The engine turns the propeller. This
makes the ship move through the water.

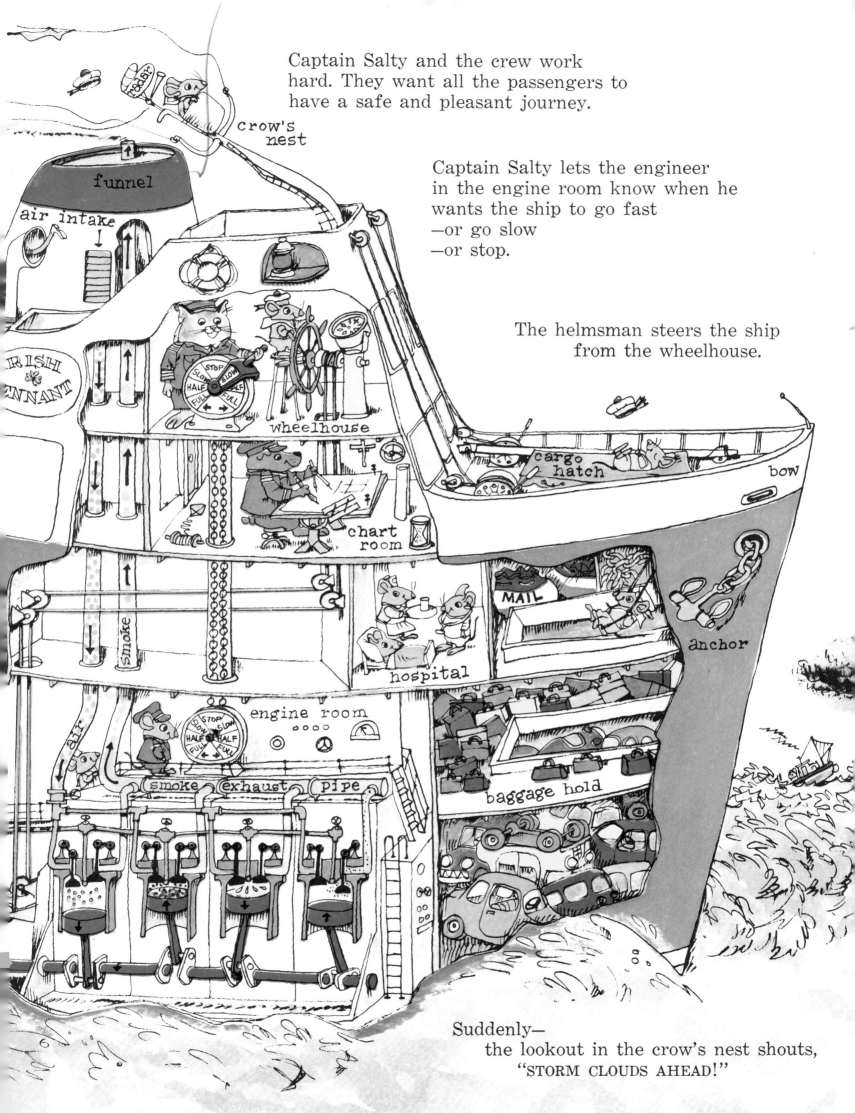

crow's nest

Captain Salty and the crew work hard. They want all the passengers to have a safe and pleasant journey.

Captain Salty lets the engineer in the engine room know when he wants the ship to go fast
—or go slow
—or stop.

The helmsman steers the ship from the wheelhouse.

funnel

air intake

IRISH PENNANT

STOP SLOW SLOW HALF HALF FULL FULL

wheelhouse

chart room

cargo hatch

bow

smoke

hospital

MAIL

anchor

air

engine room

STOP SLOW SLOW HALF HALF FULL FULL

smoke exhaust pipe

baggage hold

Suddenly—
   the lookout in the crow's nest shouts,
      "STORM CLOUDS AHEAD!"

The storm hits the ship with great fury!
The radio operator hears someone calling
on the radio.
"SOS! HELP! SAVE US! OUR BOAT IS SINKING!"

Look! There it is!
It's a small fishing boat in trouble!

"FULL SPEED AHEAD!"
roars Captain Salty.
My, the sea is rough!

LOWER THE LIFEBOAT!
Hurry! Hurry! The fishing boat is sinking!
Sailors Miff and Mo row to the rescue.

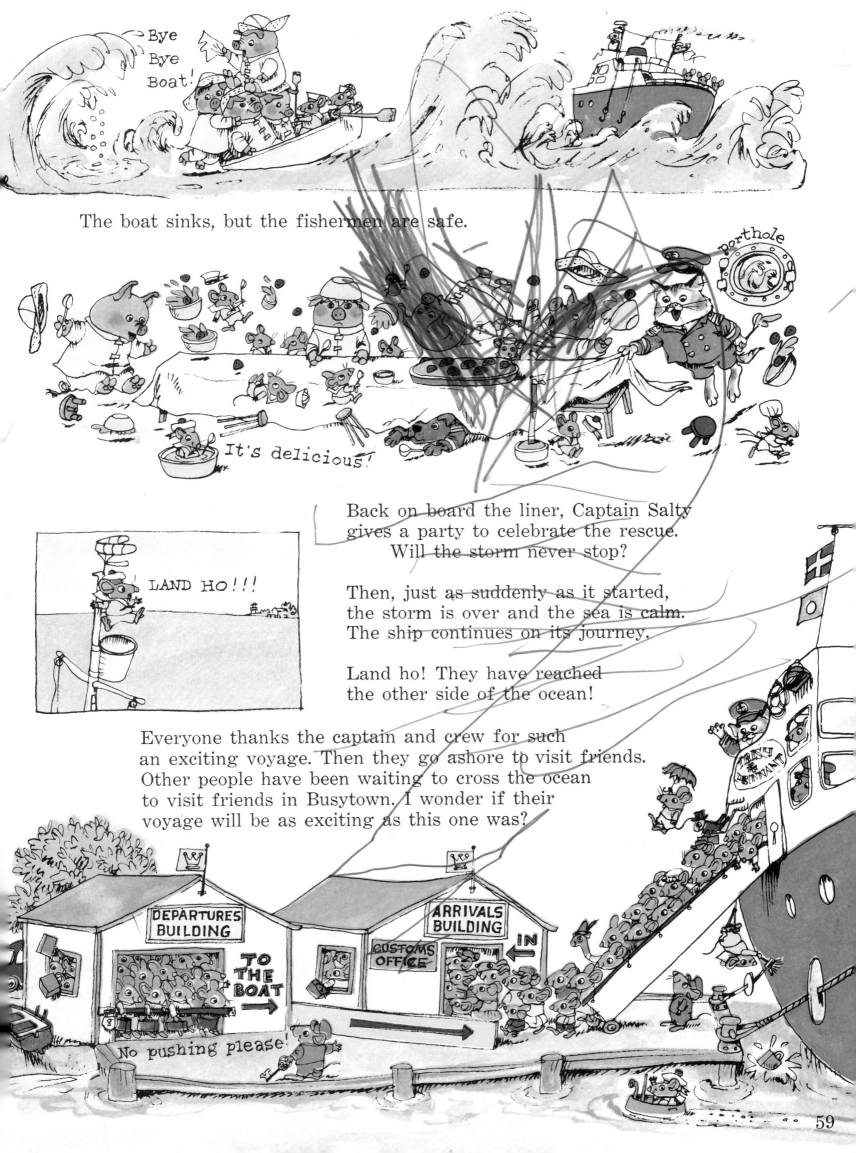

Bye
Bye
Boat!

The boat sinks, but the fishermen are safe.

It's delicious!

LAND HO!!!

Back on board the liner, Captain Salty
gives a party to celebrate the rescue.
Will the storm never stop?

Then, just as suddenly as it started,
the storm is over and the sea is calm.
The ship continues on its journey.

Land ho! They have reached
the other side of the ocean!

Everyone thanks the captain and crew for such
an exciting voyage. Then they go ashore to visit friends.
Other people have been waiting to cross the ocean
to visit friends in Busytown. I wonder if their
voyage will be as exciting as this one was?

porthole

DEPARTURES
BUILDING

ARRIVALS
BUILDING

CUSTOMS
OFFICE

TO
THE
BOAT

IN

No pushing please!

# Where bread comes from

grain combine

chaff

wheat field

wheat grain seeds

Farmer Pig gathers his crop of wheat with a harvesting machine. The grain seeds are separated from the stalks and poured into a truck.

bucket loader

The wheat grain seeds are scooped out and put into bags.

Then the seeds are taken to the mill.

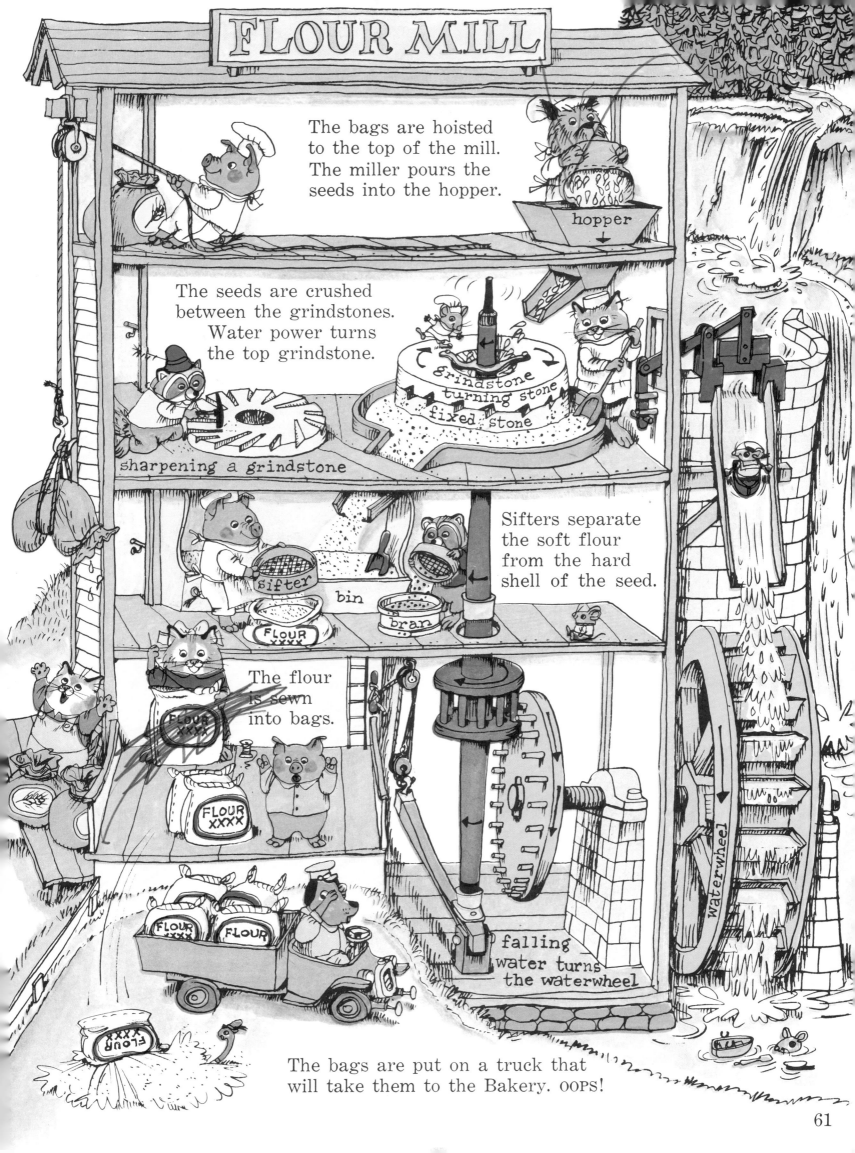

# FLOUR MILL

The bags are hoisted to the top of the mill. The miller pours the seeds into the hopper.

hopper

The seeds are crushed between the grindstones. Water power turns the top grindstone.

grindstone
turning stone
fixed stone

sharpening a grindstone

Sifters separate the soft flour from the hard shell of the seed.

sifter

bin

bran

FLOUR XXXX

The flour is sewn into bags.

FLOUR XXXX

FLOUR XXXX

falling water turns the waterwheel

waterwheel

FLOUR XXXX    FLOUR

The bags are put on a truck that will take them to the Bakery. OOPS!

The bakers will bake the flour into bread.

mixing trough

They mix water and salt and yeast with the flour to make bread dough. It is important to mix the right amounts. The yeast makes the dough puff up. The bakers knead the dough until it is well mixed.

Able Baker Charlie mixes his own special dough. Isn't he putting too much yeast in his dough?

The bakers mold the dough into loaves of many different shapes and sizes.

Able Baker Charlie has made teeny tiny loaves.

Baker Fox cleans the hot fire coals out of the ovens.